RAILROAD TIES

ROSE MARIE MEUWISSEN

Bernice,
Enjoy
Rose Marie
Meuwissen

Railroad Ties
Digital/Print Edition

https://www.rosemariemeuwissen.com

NO GHOSTWRITERS WERE USED IN THE CREATION OF THIS BOOK. THIS WORK OF FICTION IS 100% THE ORIGINAL WORK OF ROSE MARIE MEUWISSEN.

ISBN: 978-0-9903788-7-7
Published in the United States of America
Nordic Publishing
Edited by Ursula Avery
Cover Design by Rose Marie Meuwissen
Cover Photo by Jeffrey Comfort

Created with Vellum

To Dennis and his love of trains that he has shared with me through the years.

A MINNESOTA LAKES ROMANCE NOVELETTE

Lake Superior

INTRODUCTION

Kayla—

It was time Kayla started living her life again, however visiting Two Harbors, a small town in Northern Minnesota, to see the brilliant fall colors and staying at a train hotel, probably wasn't one of her best decisions.

Little did Kayla know, by following her late husband's love of trains to the shores of Lake Superior, she would end up on the right track to fall in love again.

Josh—

Being a single parent took up most of Josh's day, leaving little time for him to even think about trying to meet a woman who would be interested in a man with a child. His only goal on the trip to Lake Superior was to share his love of trains with his son.

But when fate deals him a chance at love again, will he be able to open his heart one more time?

LAND OF 10,000 LAKES

CHAPTER 1

Kayla Langley couldn't believe she was doing this. In fact, she was absolutely positive she didn't want to do it and it was most likely the worst idea her best friend, Sara, ever had. Every mile she drove further up north, towards Duluth, the vibrant gold and fiery reds of fall deepened and intensified. The landscape was undeniably a beautiful and amazing scene to behold since Minnesota was having one of its best years for fall colors in a long time. Unfortunately, her mind was inundated with memories of past drives up north with Kevin. He loved their yearly drive up to Duluth every September. Most years luck had been on their side and they managed to catch a sunny weekend. Today, it looked like luck was on her side again as the forecast was for sunny days with temps in the high seventies.

She saw the exit sign for Toby's restaurant in Hinkley and took the exit ramp off the freeway. One just couldn't go up to Duluth without stopping at Toby's for a cinnamon or caramel roll. Breakfast probably would be a good thing since she'd only had a bottle of water so far this morning.

Eating alone in a restaurant wasn't something she liked to

do, but since her husband, Kevin, lost his battle with pancreatic cancer two years ago, she'd learned to be okay with it. Her eyes watered for a moment as she remembered the many times they'd walked into Toby's restaurant together. *Why was she doing this?* She knew this trip would stir up memories of Kevin and she was completely unsure how this was going to help her get over him. Losing Kevin still hurt and she wasn't sure it would ever stop hurting.

"Here's your caramel roll all heated up, nice and warm," the waitress said as she set the plate down.

"Thanks," Kayla answered and mustered up a smile. The caramel had melted and the butter, she placed on the top of the roll, quickly melted and ran down the sides. She took a bite and was swept away in the moment as her taste buds enjoyed the scrumptious flavor of mingling caramel and cinnamon. Of course, there was no way she could eat the whole thing as Toby's was known for their generous portions. No, Kevin was not there to eat his half so she would take it with her and save it for breakfast tomorrow or a snack later on.

Back on the road again, she listened to her favorite songs and tried to figure out just what she was going to do once she got to Duluth. In her bag, she had a couple of books to read—the actual paper kind. Her Kindle was also in the bag loaded with more E-books to read. It was the new tech age so she'd purchased the E-reader, but she still preferred to hold a print book in her hands while she read. Old habits just seemed to die hard. Her plan was to relax, read and get started writing her next book. But, what she was going to write about, she had no idea. Hopefully, she would come up with something this weekend.

CHAPTER 2

Kayla had a reservation at the Northern Rail Traincar Inn, just off Lake Superior on Lake Shore Scenic Drive near Two Harbors. It was a hotel Kevin had mentioned and they'd planned to make a reservation to stay there the next year. But, he got sick and they hadn't made it back up to the North Shore again. Kevin loved trains, both small model trains and the large actual locomotives, and the Northern Rail Traincar Inn consisted of authentic train boxcars, complete with graffiti, connected by a walkway and converted into hotel rooms. *Why had she let Sara talk her into this?* Staying there was only going to make her feel more sad and alone. What she really needed to do was cancel the reservation and stay in a hotel back in Duluth. But then, she would lose her deposit, so she just needed to work through it.

It was lunchtime when she pulled into Duluth, so she stopped down at the Duluth Boardwalk area, parked close to the shops and restaurants so she could do a little shopping after lunch before driving the rest of the way to Two Harbors.

It was a beautiful sunny day and actually warm even with the cool wind blowing in off Lake Superior. Ivar's food truck stood parked along the Boardwalk selling fish and chips so she placed an order. She found an empty bench with a view of the lakefront where she could watch the boats coming and going and sat down to eat. Her heart broke as she watched the couples walking by holding hands, smiling at each other. She needed to move on. Her friends told her to, along with her grief counselor, but her heart kept saying no, not yet. But, deep down she knew it was time. She wanted to feel happy again. She wanted to feel all the pleasures and joys of being in love again. But, she couldn't even imagine where in the world she was going to find another man who could make her feel happy enough to love again. She had absolutely no idea where to begin. Maybe once she decided she was ready to move on, she would find that special man, since it always helped to be looking. At least it couldn't hurt. Right?

After eating lunch, she purchased a few things in the quaint boutique shops along the boardwalk. With her new found treasures in hand, she walked back to her car. She left the parking lot and merged onto the Lake Shore drive to Two Harbors. The houses lining this scenic drive were a combination of old and new world. Some were mansions from a bygone era and some were new ones built according to today's standards with six car garages, swimming pools, and guesthouses. They were all magnificent and pristine.

A little bit further out of town, the road split into the bypass highway or the scenic lakeshore drive. She opted for the latter. Heck, she wasn't in any hurry, so she decided on the road with awesome views of Lake Superior and the incredible fall colors. The two roads joined again right before entering Two Harbors. Highway 61 went right through town and was lined with shops—boutiques, antique stores, touristy stores, bars and restaurants. Kayla debated on stopping to shop, but decided to keep going and get checked into the hotel first. She could always come back later when she became bored, which wasn't going to take much.

She only had a few more miles to go since she had just passed Betty's Pies. Their parking lot was full which confirmed their popularity among the tourists to the area. It was still early, but she was definitely going to have dinner there later. Finally, she saw the sign for the entrance into the Northern Rail Traincar Inn. She drove down the long driveway and pulled up by the front door. The hotel was made out of two rows of actual train boxcars resting on real railroad tracks and hooked together with a hallway down the center. Kevin would've loved this place. No sense sitting out in the car feeling sorry for herself and Kevin, so she got out of the car and went inside to check in.

"Welcome," said the man at the front desk.

Kayla handed him her reservation print out and he proceeded to check her in. "Thanks," she said taking her key card and receipt.

CHAPTER 3

There was a bookshelf in the lobby filled with books and she was drawn to it by her love of books and writing, so she walked over to take a look. It was filled with children's books and adult novels, mostly ones portraying Lake Superior and Northern Minnesota. She flipped through a couple, but it only made her feel guilty knowing she hadn't done any writing since Kevin was diagnosed with cancer, three years ago. When they found out he wouldn't make it, she felt compelled to spend all her time with him, consequently she hadn't written.

She couldn't write, not when she was surrounded by pain and anger. Anger about the cards dealt her. But, now it was time to start writing again. In fact, that was one of the main reasons she'd decided to come to Two Harbors on the North Shore of Lake Superior, she badly needed some inspiration to jump-start her writing. She knew one day she wanted to write a story about Kevin and his heroic fight against cancer, but now wasn't the time. No, she needed to write about something happy and what she really needed to do was feel like love was still a possibility, because how else was she ever going to be able to write another romance novel? Especially one with a happy ending?

Deep in thought, she made her way towards the door so she could park her car and get her bags. Just then, she walked right smack into a rock hard manly chest that smelled so good she wanted to lay her head right down on it. She felt strong hands on her arms gently pushing her back away from the little bit of heaven she'd just landed on.

"Sorry, ma'am," he said staring down into her bright blue eyes.

"No, my fault, I wasn't paying attention," Kayla said looking up into his warm brown eyes and a beautiful smile revealing perfect and straight white teeth. He was about six feet tall, at least five inches taller than her, muscular with short-cropped dark brown hair. Her body had reacted boldly on its own to this man and she could still feel the fire in the pit of her stomach. *What was wrong with her?* It had been way too long since she'd been with a man, that's what was wrong. Apparently her body knew what it needed even if her head didn't. She backed away a little more, totally at a loss for words.

"Dad, wait for me." The wood door opened and a young boy about ten years old came running through the open door and stopped right behind the man.

"Hi," the boy said. "I'm Tanner. What's your name?" He walked around to stand in front of his dad.

At a loss of how to get out of introductions, she answered, "I'm Kayla. Happy to meet you." She held out her hand and the boy extended his hand to shake hers. She looked back up to the man who was staring at her.

"I'm Josh. Tanner's dad. Nice to meet you. The two of us are spending a few days up here to check out some special trains in the area. Are you checking in or out?"

"In," she answered. Kayla noticed him looking at her ring

finger where she still wore her wedding rings. *Damn!* She should've never been wearing them. They should be at home or at the very least on the other hand. She'd already noticed he didn't have a ring on. Probably divorced. *What the Hell was she doing?*

"Well, we'll probably see you around here then." He took Tanner's hand and they walked past her to the front desk to check in.

"Probably." Kayla smiled and walked out the door of the hotel.

She got into her car and moved it to the parking lot. *What an idiot she was!* She was so intent on not moving on, she was still wearing her wedding rings. If you weren't looking, it just didn't matter, that was why, and she hadn't been looking up until a few minutes ago. This was her weekend to get her act back together and move on. She should've left the rings at home. The diamond sparkled in the sunlight. She loved the ring, it was a part of her. No, it was a symbol of *their* marriage, *their* life together. It was over though. He was gone. She slipped the rings off her finger and put them carefully and lovingly inside the zippered compartment in her purse. There. She'd done it. She was going to move on. Hopefully, it wasn't too late. She got out, opened the trunk and took out her suitcases. As she closed the trunk, she heard a truck drive up beside her. It was Josh and Tanner.

Josh got out and walked towards her. "Just wanted to apologize for walking into you earlier. You are a really beautiful woman. . . Any guy would find you attractive. . .You caught me off guard. I noticed the wedding ring afterwards."

"I'm not."

"Not?" Josh asked looking at her ring finger now bare.

"I'm a widow. Just hadn't had a reason to take them off before."

"We're good then?" he asked.

"Josh's mother?" Kayla asked.

"I'm divorced," he stated.

"We're good then," she smiled.

The truck door closed and Tanner stood next to his dad. "I'm getting hungry. When are we going to go eat?"

"A little later."

"I'm going to get settled in. See you later." Kayla nodded and walked back into the lobby.

"Later," Josh said as she walked away.

CHAPTER 4

Kayla got everything put away in her room, the whole time wondering how he was going to see her later if he didn't know her room number.

She took out her laptop and powered it up. A writer always had a file folder full of one page story ideas which was probably the best place to find an idea to get started writing again. She picked one titled, *Heating up the Glacier,* about falling in love on a train ride to Glacier Park in Montana. One about trains. Yes, that would work. After reading the first page of ideas for the story, she started writing. A couple of hours later, she could no longer put up with her rumbling stomach. Betty's Pies was calling her name.

The parking lot was still full, when she pulled into a parking spot around five. Josh's car was still parked in the spot next to her when she left, leaving no chance of running into him again. She put her name on the list and sat down on a bench in the lobby to wait. The twenty minute wait passed slowly while she sat on the bench alone observing the other people waiting. Mostly couples, in fact, she was the only one who was alone. She hated this the most. The eating alone at restaurants. It made her want to get in her car and just go home. Her number, 59, was next though, so she would just wait, mainly because she was famished. She got up to look at the pies in the glass case. The pies looked absolutely enticing, she could hardly wait to taste the rhubarb custard pie.

"Kayla."

She heard her name and turned around to see Tanner walking quickly towards her. "Hi," she said and saw Josh walking towards her also.

"Doesn't surprise me to see you here, since it is the only restaurant near the hotel," Josh said and walked over to the counter to get a number. Number 80.

"59," the hostess at the counter shouted to be heard.

Kayla heard her number called and walked over to the counter. "Can I change that to three?"

"Of course, the table seats four anyway," the hostess said.

"Just a moment," Kayla said and walked over to Josh and Tanner. "Would you guys like to join me for dinner? My table is ready now and then you wouldn't have to wait. I'd love the company."

Josh smiled, "Sure, thanks."

The three of them followed the waitress to a table. They ordered quickly. Kayla wasn't sure what she'd just gotten herself into but Josh was definitely a hunk. "What do you do, Josh, besides like trains?"

"I'm the Mesaba Division Supervisor for the Canadian National Railroad. I oversee all the train operations on the Mesaba Iron Range in northern Minnesota. How about you?" Josh asked.

"I'm a writer."

"Wow, didn't think people could really make a living doing that."

"Some people do. I haven't put anything new out in the last couple of years though," she answered.

"I like to draw," Tanner said. "I'll show you some of my stuff later at the hotel."

"I'd love to see it," Kayla said. "I've thought about writing a children's book, but I would never attempt the illustrations. I'm awful at drawing."

"So what do you write?" Josh asked.

"Promise you won't laugh?" she asked.

Josh nodded.

"Romance novels."

"Really? Wow." Josh searched her face for what she wasn't sure. He was silent for a few moments, and then said, "I'd like to read one of your books sometime. You'll have to tell me your last name though. Or do you write under a different name? I heard some people do that."

"My last name is Langley, but I use my maiden name. Kayla Winters."

"Dad, can I read her book, too?" Tanner asked.

"My books are just for adults, Tanner."

"Oh," Tanner said.

Dinner tasted absolutely delicious and the rhubarb custard pie was so scrumptious it satisfied every taste bud's anticipation. Tanner talked non-stop with Josh offering more info about his job.

They got up to leave and Josh picked up the tab, "I got this."

"You don't have to do that."

"Of course, I do. You let us butt in line and saved us at least a half hour of waiting for a table."

"Okay, if you insist," she said as they walked out to their cars.

CHAPTER 5

Walking back into the hotel, Tanner ran in ahead of them.

Josh stopped walking, so Kayla did also.

"I'd like to spend more time talking to you. After Tanner goes to bed, would you meet me at the hot tub?" Josh asked.

"Sure, what time?" Kayla asked.

"Does ten work?" Josh asked.

"Yes, I'll see you then."

Back in her room, Kayla was as excited as a high school girl. *What was she thinking to agree to meet a new man in her swimming suit?* Swimsuits just laid it all out there. She wasn't apprehensive about her figure, no, that was definitely not a concern, but still a swimsuit was a little bit too little. Her dark red hair fell past her shoulders and she needed to decide whether to leave it down or put it up for the hot tub. She decided on up in a brown clip.

She'd never been overweight, in fact, she'd lost weight through Kevin's whole cancer ordeal. After Kevin died, eating had lost its appeal. Today had been different though, she actually was hungry and enjoyed the meal. Especially the pie. Josh would like what he saw and for some reason she really wanted him to. It came back to that old thing called chemistry and she certainly felt it with Josh.

At ten she slid the cover-up over her bikini, walked down to the lobby and outside to the hot tub. The temp had dropped to sixty, but the sky was clear and filled with stars. It always amazed her how much brighter the stars were in northern Minnesota, especially once you got out of the cities. Even though she couldn't see Lake Superior, she knew it lay just behind the trees and road. She could faintly hear the waves lapping the shore. She saw Josh in the hot tub waiting for her. Slowly the cover-up dropped to the ground, she reached down, picked it up and laid it on a chair. For now, they had the hot tub to themselves. The water was hot, but comfortable considering the air temp. She could feel his eyes watching her as she entered the water, she smiled at him.

"Glad you came," Josh said.

"I said I would," Kayla answered sitting down across from him, mainly because she was extremely nervous and way too scared to sit next to him. Besides, it would be easier to talk to him this way.

"Tanner wanted to come along, but I told him it was adult time now."

"Was he okay with that?" she asked.

"Not really, but he knew he wasn't going to get to come, so he went to bed."

"This is really awkward," Kayla said watching his eyes looking at her and a huge smile spread across his face.

"That's because we don't know each other yet, so tell me about yourself. How long have you been writing?" Josh asked.

"Oh, probably my whole life. I was first published about ten years ago. I have an English degree from the University of Minnesota. What else can you do with an English degree besides write or teach? I'm not cut out to teach and I have so many stories in my head needing to be written."

"I googled you and found you have an impressive list of published books. I think I may have to read my first romance novel," Josh laughed.

"As a guy, you probably would like one of my contemporary novels best."

"I'll keep that in mind, while choosing one."

"What exactly do you do for the railroad as a division supervisor?" Kayla asked.

"I oversee all the train movements on the Mesaba Range, mainly involving transporting ore from the mines to the ore docks on Lake Superior in Two Harbors and Duluth. I grew up around trains and have always liked anything to do with them. That's one of the main reasons we are staying at this hotel. In case you hadn't noticed, it's made out of train cars." Josh pointed back to the hotel train cars.

"I had noticed," she laughed.

"And tomorrow an old World War II steam engine, The 261, will be pulling into Two Harbors. Tanner likes trains, too. Like father, like son, as they say. He hasn't seen a real steam engine fired up and pulling a train before. It is a sight to see, just like out of the old movies."

"I'd like to see it. I've always been a fan of the old movies and the ones with trains usually have romances in them," she said smiling coyly.

"I see. Maybe you'd like to join us tomorrow?" Josh asked.

"Maybe," she answered.

The jets on the hot tub stopped. Josh got out to reset the timer. Seconds later, he was sitting on her side of the tub. She was getting too hot so she got up and sat on the edge of the tub.

"This may be a little forward, but what happened to Tanner's mother?" Kayla asked.

"She became pregnant when we were dating, so we got married, but she was a wild one and after Tanner was born she tried to be a wife and mother for a couple of years. It just wasn't her thing to be married, much less be a mother. She divorced me and gave me full custody of Tanner. She never liked the cold winters here, so she said she was going to California. Haven't heard from her since. "

"Oh, I'm sorry. It must've been hard to be a single dad all these years. And it must be hard on Tanner to have no contact with his mother," Kayla said and slipped back into the water, as she was chilled now.

"All I can do is be the best Dad I can. We do pretty good. My mother helps me a lot with Tanner. She lives in Duluth, too." Josh turned to face her. "Can I ask about your husband?"

"Kevin. We met in college and married after graduation. He liked trains, too. We had, actually still have, a model railroad in the basement of our house in Forest Lake. My house now. He got pancreatic cancer about three years ago. There really isn't much you can do to fight it, but we tried the chemo, which gave him another six months. He's been gone now for two years." Tears filled her eyes as she talked. "I'm sorry, it still hurts to lose someone you were planning on spending the rest of your life with."

"I'm sorry. You didn't say anything about children?" Josh asked reaching over to place his hand over her hand resting on the edge of the tub.

"We hadn't got to it yet. We wanted to. We talked about it, but then he got sick."

CHAPTER 6

Josh brought his other hand up under her chin and their lips met in a kiss. His lips moved slowly over hers and then he deepened the kiss. She responded with every fiber of her being, as her arm went around his neck. It felt good and it had been a long time since she'd felt this kind of pleasure. At least two years. Josh ended the kiss.

She stared into his eyes and became lost to the fire burning in them and inside her. She stood up, stepped out of the hot tub and wrapped a towel around her now chilled body.

Josh got out, grabbed his towel, and wiped off the dripping water from his body. He stood in front of her. "I didn't mean to scare you off."

"No, you didn't. Never was a fan of sex in the hot tub." She smiled and watched Josh's face for signs of approval. He smiled back at her. "I'm in room 220. See you in 15 minutes?"

"You got it!" Josh said and they walked back inside. He left her at her door.

Kayla stripped, dried off and threw on the cover up. This

was daring. Josh was a good man, she could tell by the way he'd raised Tanner. He was unbelievably good looking, and the attraction was so strong she wasn't going to bother fighting it. Hell, she'd been with a couple of other guys before she met Kevin, it would be fine. She heard a knock at the door, walked over and opened the door. Josh stood there dressed in jean shorts and a button down short-sleeved shirt, he hadn't bothered to button, wearing a huge grin on his face. He stepped inside and shut the door behind him.

As soon as the door shut, he pulled her into his arms, where she went willingly. His lips descended on hers in a soul-searching kiss devouring both of them. Minutes later, they were lying on the bed wrapped in each other's arms, he was kissing her neck and his hands reached up to cup her breast. She felt the recognition in his hand when he realized she didn't have anything on underneath the cover up dress, which heightened her response. His hand moved to the hem of the cover up dress sliding it upwards, and she felt his finger slide smoothly inside her as her body arched into his touch. Her orgasm came quickly.

The cover up dress slid further up and over her head. She watched him stand to remove his shorts revealing he too hadn't bothered to put anything on underneath them. His hand slid into his pocket removing a condom which he slid on quickly. He was ready, that was apparent. She waited anticipating his entry into her body. His chest was hovering over hers as his lips suckled her breasts one at a time, then moved to her lips as she felt him seeking entrance. He moved slowly in and out, gradually building speed until she cried out and minutes later so did he. He pulled out slowly and moved beside her on the bed. She surveyed every inch of his naked body as he came to lie next to her. *Oh, how she liked what she saw!* Sex with him had met her every expectation. It was a bit quick, but she was in a hurry this time too, since it had been way too long.

"Sorry, that was so quick," he said gently brushing a stray hair from her face. "It's been a while since I've slept with a woman. Next time we'll take our time."

"It's been at least two years for me. I don't think I would've been able to take my time either. Not this time, but next time would be good."

Josh got up and put his shorts back on and Kayla slipped her cover up dress over her head.

"I have to go back to the room. Tanner. Sometimes being a dad has its drawbacks." He put his shirt on and walked to the door.

Kayla followed him to the door. "What time are we leaving to go see The 261?"

Josh smiled, pulled her against his chest and kissed her. "Ten. See you in the lobby tomorrow morning."

CHAPTER 7

Kayla watched him walk down the hall to his room and shut the door. She lay down on the bed and smiled. She'd done it. She'd taken the first step, actually, it was a big step, to moving on. It had felt great, everything she remembered it could be between a man and a woman. It would be a package deal, though, and was she ready to be a mom? She really hadn't thought about it before. She'd always wanted to have children, but a ten-year-old boy. *Could she do it?* Tanner seemed to like her. That was a plus. But the biggest plus was it appeared Josh liked her.

At ten in the morning, she watched Josh and Tanner walk down the hall to meet her. She'd debated the whole morning whether she should drive her own car or ride with them. Heck, she'd just had sex with the guy. She should be able to trust him enough to get in his car. *Right?*

"Ready?" Josh asked.

"Ready. Can't wait to see this steam engine," Kayla said as she watched Tanner's face filled with excitement to go and see the train.

"Me, too," Tanner said and walked up to her taking her hand. "I'm glad you're going with us. I like you, Kayla."

Fifteen minutes later they pulled into Two Harbors' train station's parking lot. The lot was full of families with small children and other train enthusiasts milling about everywhere.

"I brought my paper notebook along. I'm going to draw the train when it gets here," Tanner said to Kayla as they walked towards the platform to wait with the crowd.

"I'm glad you came. I hope you won't be bored," Josh said.

"Not a chance. I'm going to use a train in the story I'm working on, so this will be good writing research," she answered. "Besides, I like your company."

"See the steam down that way, it's coming," Josh said to Tanner while pointing toward the train just rounding the curve in the tracks.

The jet-black, massive, old world, steam engine proudly thundered along the tracks leaving a trail of billowing steam and smoke in its wake. It exuded power as if it was a living and breathing black stallion galloping into town. Lake Superior's sky blue water glistened in the bright sun a few yards away. A totally impressive scene and one she would definitely have to use in a story some time. She was glad to be here with this man and boy who'd literally just walked into her life.

The 261 engine shuddered to a stop at the station and Tanner pulled out his paper and began drawing the proud 261 engine. His concentration was impressive as his pencil flew across the paper.

It was very good. He was talented, that was apparent. Maybe the children's book, she'd always wanted to write, was going to happen. How perfect it would be for her to write a children's story about trains to honor Kevin's love of model trains along with Josh and Tanner's love of real trains. She could even have Tanner draw the train pictures for it.

Josh had been talking to the train engineer and now came over to stand beside her. He effortlessly put his arm around her and casually pulled her to him.

"I never gave much thought to all the stuff about love at first sight, but I know I could definitely fall in love with you. Where do you want to go from here?" Josh asked. His face revealed the sincerity of his confession.

"I think that may be a good starting point. You, falling in love with me, that is. And, I think I could easily fall in love with you, too," Kayla said wearing her heart on her sleeve.

"We may live a few miles apart, but I think it's totally doable," Josh said.

"I can do my writing from anywhere, so I don't see location as a problem," Kayla said and leaned into him as his lips met hers. It was her time to move on and she was finally ready.

Thank God for trains! They'd brought Kevin years of pleasure and now they would hopefully be a part of her new life, too. Along with these two special men, Josh and Tanner.

AUTHOR'S NOTE

As a child I spent many summers staying at my grandma's home, which happened to be above her restaurant, in a small town in northern Minnesota where the railroad tracks were literally in her backyard.

When I was nine years old, my mother took me to California on a train, and in the seventies I travelled to Norway and also visited Sweden by taking the train from Oslo to Stockholm.

I've spent the last 20 years with a man who loves trains of all sizes whether they are HO scale model trains or full size trains we can travel on like the Empire builder passenger cars pulled by the 261 Steam engine. Over the years, we've traveled on the Amtrak Empire builder from Minneapolis to Seattle, the Norway in a Nutshell train from Bergen to Oslo, the Branson Scenic Railway and the North Shore Scenic Railway from Duluth to Two Harbors.

In our travels we are constantly stopping to visit anything Scandinavian or related to trains! If you're looking for a unique hotel experience check out the Northern Rail

Traincar Inn, from the story, made out of actual train cars, I highly recommend it.

I hope reading my story provided a look into the train world and that everyone has the opportunity to ride the rails someday.

RHUBARB CUSTARD PIE

Makes one 9-inch pie

Crust

1 -9 inch Pie Crust (unbaked)

Pie filling

1 1/4 cups sugar
1/4 teaspoon salt
3 tablespoons flour
2 eggs, beaten
4 cups rhubarb, chopped into small pieces

Topping

1/2 cup sugar
1/2 cup flour
1/2 cup butter
1 pinch salt

Preheat the oven at 350 degrees.

Stir together the dry ingredients for the filling. Stir in the beaten eggs, then add the chopped rhubarb and mix all together.

Pour into unbaked pie shell.

Topping: Mix together the sugar and flour in a small bowl. Using a fork, cut in the butter until the mixture becomes "crumbly". Sprinkle topping mixture over the rhubarb filling.

Bake for one hour at 350 degrees.

PIE PHOTO

Rhubarb Custard Pie

ABOUT THE AUTHOR

ROSE MARIE MEUWISSEN

Rose Marie Meuwissen, a first-generation Norwegian American born and raised in Minnesota, always tries to incorporate her Norwegian heritage into her writing. After receiving a BA in Marketing from Concordia University, a Masters in Creative Writing from Hamline University soon followed. Minnesota is still where she calls home.

She has traveled around the world, including Scandinavia, but still has many places to see, enjoys attending Scandinavian events, writing conferences and is usually busy writing Minnesota Lakes Contemporary Romances, Viking Time Travel Romances or Norwegian Traditions Children's Books.

Visit her at www.rosemariemeuwissen.com or www.realnorwegianseatlutefisk.com.

NOVELS

- ***Taking Chances***—a contemporary romance novel set in Minnesota and Arizona.
- ***Married by Saturday***—a contemporary romance novel set in Minnesota and Montana.
- ***Looking for Mr. Right***—a contemporary internet dating romance novel set on Prior Lake in Minnesota—***Coming soon!***

NOVELLAS

- ***Annika—A Christmas Romance***—a contemporary romance set in Minnesota with a Nordic theme during the Christmas Holidays.
- ***Skol! Viking Blonde Ale***—a contemporary romance set in Minnesota at an Autumn festival complete with a fortune teller, ale and Vikings!
- ***Choosing to Live***—a Norwegian woman's journey during WWII to survive the Nazi Occupation of Norway—***Coming soon!***

MINNESOTA LAKES ROMANCE NOVELETTES

- ***A Kiss Under the Northern Lights***—a Summer romance set in Ely, Minnesota on Big Lake.
- ***Dancing in the Moonlight***—a Summer romance set in Malmo, Minnesota on Mille Lacs Lake.
- ***Hot Summer Nights***—a Summer romance set in Prior Lake, Minnesota on Prior Lake.
- ***Railroad Ties***—an Autumn romance set in Two Harbors, Minnesota on Lake Superior.
- ***Blizzard of Love***—a Winter romance set in Lutsen, Minnesota on Lake Superior.
- ***Nor-Way to Love***—a Spring romance set in Minneapolis, Minnesota on Lake Harriet.
- ***Old Yule Log Fires***—a Christmas romance set in Excelsior, Minnesota on Lake Minnetonka.
- ***A Date for Valentine's Day***—a Valentine romance set in Minnetonka Beach, Minnesota at the Lafayette Country Club on Lake Minnetonka.
- ***Dance of Love***—a Fall Festival romance set at the Renaissance Fair in Shakopee, Minnesota.

CHILDREN'S BOOKS—REAL NORWEGIAN'S SERIES

- ***Real Norwegians Eat Lutefisk***—a Children's book about the tradition of Lutefisk presented in both English and Norwegian.
- ***Real Norwegians Eat Rømmegrøt***—the second Children's book in the series about the tradition of Rømmegrøt presented in both English and Norwegian.
- ***Real Norwegians Eat Lefse***—the third Children's book in the series about the tradition of Lefse presented in both English and Norwegian.
- ***Real Norwegians Eat Krumkake***—the fourth Children's book in the series about the tradition of Krumkake presented in both English and Norwegian—***Coming next!***

MICRO-MINI NOVELETTE—COMING SOON!

- ***Christmas Notes***—a collection of Christmas prose poems to warm the heart during the Christmas season.

CONTINUE READING FOR A PREVIEW OF:

SKOL! VIKING BLONDE ALE

Fortunes, Love & Fate Series

SKOL! VIKING BLONDE ALE

COVER

COPYRIGHT—SKOL! VIKING BLONDE ALE

FORTUNES, LOVE & FATE SERIES

Print Edition

NO GHOSTWRITERS WERE USED IN THE CREATION OF THIS BOOK. This work of fiction is 100% the original work of Rose Marie Meuwissen.

ISBN 978-0-9903788-3-9

Published in the United States of America
Nordic Publishing LLC
Cover Design by Raine English

SKOL! VIKING BLONDE ALE

FORTUNES, LOVE & FATE SERIES

Inga was living the dream, planning events for her own company, Unique Events, but she still hadn't found a guy who could be 'The One' for her. She never would've believed a fortune from a gypsy fortune teller promising her a 'love that surpasses time' could come true.

Erik moved from Norway to Minnesota to expand his Nordic Brewing company in the U. S. He'd promised himself to devote all his time to the business, but how was he to know that an unknown force of fate would introduce him to a woman he couldn't walk away from?

Their attraction could not be denied because ultimately, they were destined to be together. But could the Atlantic Ocean keep them apart? Would that even be possible if they were truly soul mates?

INGA'S FORTUNE:

Someone from your past will reappear in your life.
Your true soul mate.
With him, you will experience a love that surpasses time.

PROLOGUE

James J. Hill Days in Wayzata on Lake Minnetonka
September

Inga pulled into the back-parking lot of Main Street Books at six. She couldn't believe it wasn't later. Friday night rush hour traffic on the 494 Freeway was bumper to bumper all the way from Eden Prairie to Wayzata. The weather was still holding its summer like temps and true Minnesotans would never pass up a beautiful autumn weekend to go up North to their cabins one last time before winter arrived. Today was the James J. Hill Days celebration in Wayzata and the main street was packed with people as she made her way into the book store to find her *Romancing the Lakes of Minnesota* book club. This month instead of their regular meeting, they planned to enjoy walking around and checking out the celebration. Probably was a good call, she thought, since it would've been difficult to hold their meeting in the crowded book store and the activity outside would've been immensely distracting.

"Am I the last one to arrive?" Inga asked as she approached the book club group standing in front of the latest arrival shelf where the romance section was located.

"Bet the traffic was awful," Nora stated.

"Ready, to brave the crowds?" Katie asked.

"I'm hungry and thirsty, let's go!" Violet said.

Inga nodded in agreement and followed the group out the door to Main Street. They made their way down the street stopping at booths to look at the novelties for sale until finally, they stopped at the end of the street where the most unusual trailer was parked. The sign above the open door read, 'Fortune Teller'. It appeared to be Vintage, but these days they could make anything look old, even if it was new. Although, she had to admit, she'd never seen anything like it before, even though she'd been to many events. After all, she was an event planner. Intrigued was putting it mildly. Unfortunately, there was no stopping her curiosity. So, she entered the trailer.

"Come in, please," a very thickly accented voice beckoned from inside the trailer.

"Hello." Inga ducked and stepped into the trailer, taking in all the antiques and draped surroundings.

"Take a seat," the lady in gypsy like garb directed. "Let me see what your life has in store for you."

Inga didn't believe in fortune telling, at least she didn't think she did, but what could it possibly hurt to oblige the lady. It might be worth a laugh later, so she sat down on the partially pulled out chair at the table.

The fortune teller took the seat across from Inga and reached for her hand.

Slowly, Inga extended her hand. When their hands touched, Inga felt a strange sensation flow through her entire body, almost like a spark of electricity. It only lasted a few seconds and then was gone. She had no idea what it was or what caused it, but she finally relaxed.

The woman's face seemed deep in thought and completely fixated on her hand. "You are a very special lady. Very strong and independent. I see happiness in your future."

"Do you see a man?" Inga wasn't sure why'd she'd asked that particular question.

"Yes." The woman continued staring at her hand. "A very handsome man."

"Well, there certainly are enough good-looking men around. What I need is one that is interested in me long enough to stick around for a while."

"You have not met '*The One*' yet."

"When? When will it happen? I'm getting really tired of waiting around for him."

"Soon."

"So, is that my fortune?"

"No." The woman hesitated, then picked up a piece of paper and wrote a few lines down on it. She handed it to Inga. "This is your fortune: ***Someone from your past will reappear in your life. Your true soul mate. With him, you will experience a love that surpasses time."***

"Great. But I'm sorry, I don't believe in magic."

"That's okay you don't have to believe. It will happen anyway."

Their eyes locked for a moment.

Inga got up to leave. "How much do I owe you?" Inga asked.

"For you, no charge. I've been waiting for you."

"I don't understand."

The fortune teller waived her hand in a shooing motion, indicating Inga was done and should leave.

As Inga stepped out of the trailer, Katie rushed up the steps. "My turn."

"So, what do you think? Is the Fortune Teller legit?" Violet asked.

"What kind of a question is that? Of course, it's not real. No one can tell another person what will happen in their future," Stephanie said.

"Care to share?" Nora asked.

Inga handed the piece of paper to Violet, who in turn handed it to Stephanie, who in turn handed it to Gwen and lastly to Nora.

"At least it's a good fortune. Let's hope it comes true," Stephanie said.

"Come on, you're not buying into this stuff, are you?" Inga shook her head.

Minutes later, Katie came down the trailer's steps, paper in hand grinning from ear to ear.

Violet practically ran to the steps to be next.

Each romance book club member shared their fortune while the next one took their turn. Being romantics at heart, they were all thrilled to find romance in their fortunes.

They continued strolling leisurely down the other side of the street where the craft brewery tents were located.

Inga spotted a tent with *Nordic Brewing* as the name. She selected it out of the five tents because of her love for all things Nordic and Viking. In fact, the Viking Ship logo caught her eye first. She walked up to the counter to see the menu more closely.

"What can I get you?"

Inga looked up quickly when she heard the strong Norwegian accented English and to her surprise saw almost a '*Thor*' look alike, only his blonde hair was shorter. He could very well be from Viking blood, she thought. *Tall, muscular, with a chiseled face. Have I just died and gone to Valhalla?*

"What can I get you?" he repeated smiling broadly at her.

"What would you suggest?" she managed to get out. "I've never tried your brand before."

"For you lovely lady, I'd suggest the Viking Blonde Ale."

"Sounds absolutely perfect."

He turned his broad toned back toward her stretching the black T-shirt taut against his muscles and filled a plastic souvenir cup with Valhalla printed on one side and a picture of a Viking on the other side.

Inga pulled a five-dollar bill from her purse and set it on the counter. He handed her the cup instead of setting it down and her fingers lightly brushed his in the process. *There it was again.* A shiver of sorts shimmied its way through her body.

"Thank you, hope you enjoy it," he said as he picked up the money to put in the cash register.

"Thanks, I'm sure I will," Inga said while her eyes lingered on this modern-day Viking man. She felt sad that she would most likely not ever see him again. *Oh well, one can only wish.* She turned and walked away spotting her friends up ahead at a different craft brewery tent.

Made in the USA
Monee, IL
28 May 2023